Published by Age of Learning, Inc., P.O. Box 10458, Glendale, California 91209.

Library of Congress Cataloging-in-Publication Data
A Jog in the Fog/Age of Learning, Inc.
Summary: In this Word Family Beginning Reader, a dog and a hog go for a jog,
then they are guided home through the fog by a helpful frog.

ISBN: 978-1-62116-015-1
Library of Congress Control Number: 2012912296
21 20 19 18 17 16 15 14 13 12   1 2 3 4 5
Printed in the U.S.A.
First printing, December 2012

A Jog in the Fog

Age of Learning, Inc., Glendale, California
This book is also available at **ABCmouse.com**, the award-winning early learning online curriculum.
Find free apps at **ABCmouse.com/apps**.

This is a dog.

This is a hog.

The dog and the hog
go for a jog.

The dog and the hog
jog to a log.

On the log,
they see a frog!

The dog and the hog
play with the frog.

"Oh no! Look! Here comes the fog."

"We cannot see!" say
the dog and the hog.
"We cannot see
when there is fog!"

"I can help you,"
says the frog.
"I can see when
there is fog!"

"Jump off the log and come with me. Jump down when I say *One! Two! Three!*"

The dog and the hog
jump off the log.

They follow the frog
out of the fog.

"I see our home!"
says the hog to
the dog.

They say,
"Thank you!"
to the frog.

The frog says, "Goodbye!" to the dog and the hog.

The End